TOP DOG!

That's Marmaduke—the craziest excuse for a canine you'll ever shake paws with. If you're ready to laugh, sit down with huggable, hilarious Marmaduke. But leave extra room in your favorite chair—Marmaduke likes to stretch out. . . !

More Big Laughs from SIGNET

MARMADUKE® SOUNDS OFF

BRAD ANDERSON

A SIGNET BOOK

NEW AMERICAN LIBRARY

SIGNET TRADEMARK REG. U.S. PAT. OFF. AND FOREIGN COUNTRIES
REGISTERED TRADEMARK—MARCA REGISTRADA
HECHO EN CHICAGO, U.S.A.

SIGNET, SIGNET CLASSIC, MENTOR, PLUME, MERIDIAN AND
NAL BOOKS are published by New American Library,
1633 Broadway, New York, New York 10019

First Printing, July, 1985

1 2 3 4 5 6 7 8 9

PRINTED IN THE UNITED STATES OF AMERICA

"I told you not to use his doghouse
as a garage!"

5-31 © 1983 United Feature Syndicate, Inc.

"I have *not* hidden your old pillow!
I threw it out!"

BRAD ANDERSON

"It's you...it's definitely you!"

"Well, don't give it to Marmaduke if you don't like it. He won't eat it. either."

"It takes a lot of dog to turn a home
into a doghouse!"

6-3 © 1983 United Feature Syndicate, Inc.

"Oh, this is just great! You taught him to
collect aluminum cans?!"

"Look, Dad. Here comes Pac-Dog!"

"We're safe...he panhandled the pizza place!"

"Is this the dog we have to talk to
on the phone?"

"Who taught you that trick?"

"Guess what's coming to dinner."

"Now, surely you can look after them until
we get back from the vet!"

© 1983 United Feature Syndicate, Inc.

"Stop asking Marmaduke what he wants
and let him in!"

"Oh, the suffering I do to keep
him healthy."

© 1983 United Feature Syndicate, Inc.

6·16

"Mom! We'll never finish breakfast if he
keeps catching our toast!"

"You're no help!"

"Uh-oh! Here comes that
freeloader again."

"I think we'd better stop!"

"I don't know where he got it, but it says,
'Best Cat in Show!'"

"Don't let him watch! Don't let him watch!"

"This should be interesting. Let's watch
and see which way they go."

6-24 © 1983 United Feature Syndicate, Inc.   BRADANDERSON

"When you raid the cookie jar, you must
always leave at least *one* cookie!"

"I wonder who dreamed up the expression, 'work like a dog!'"

"Are you *sure* he took the pie?"

"It's like built-in radar...when he starts
jumping, the ice cream truck is on its way!"

"Hi there, Tootsie! How are you doing?"

6-29 © 1982 United Feature Syndicate, Inc. BRAD ANDERSON

"Nag, nag, nag!"

© 1983 United Feature Syndicate, Inc.

7.1

"We're one big happy family here and
it's got to stop!"

"I love you, too, but there's no steak
for you."

7.4 © 1983 United Feature Syndicate, Inc.

"Don't give me that 'when the hot dogs
disappear, why does everyone
blame me?' look!"

"I'll be glad when summer is over and he's
back to chasing school buses."

"I get a turn with Marmaduke next!"

"She's telling him she wouldn't marry him if he were the last dog on Earth."

"Why don't you dig in one spot so Phil can start a garden?"

"Would you mind parking elsewhere?"

"Stop complaining about the sign...be glad
he didn't drag home the bus!"

"I followed him home. Can he keep me?"

© 1983 United Feature Syndicate, Inc.

7.13

"Marmaduke—my hair, my hair!"

© 1983 United Feature Syndicate, Inc.

7.14

BRAD ANDERSON

"Notice how he ignores us since he found
out our police cars aren't air-conditioned."

"I don't mind him stopping the bus, but
when he gets on and greets everyone,
he throws off my schedule!"

© 1983 United Feature Syndicate, Inc.

7/16

BRAD ANDERSON

"Chewing up the bills won't help any."

"You'd better not take it to the shop. He
loves baseball and the game starts soon."

"Don't look at *me*. You're the one who
taught him to beg."

7-20

"The show ended when Marmaduke got
mad at the magician for sawing the
lady in half."

"You wouldn't dare!"

"There's someone here to see you about
your last price increase."

© 1983 United Feature Syndicate, Inc.

7-23

"Phil and Dottie never have a dull party!"

"This is what scares me about small
cars...dogs look so much bigger!"

7·26

"When I have a cold, you don't give *me* that kind of attention."

"The trouble with your pup tent is that
Marmaduke's no pup."

"Mom! There's a gentleman here
to see you!"

"Marmaduke, you were sent out here to get
him to mow the lawn!"

7-29

"I can't find my beach hat and
sunglasses anywhere!"

8-1

BRADANDERSON

"Good thing Billy loaned me
his periscope."

8-2 © 1983 United Feature Syndicate, Inc.   BRAD ANDERSON

"Marmaduke has better air conditioning
than we do, so I'm piping some of his cool
air into our house."

"Dad, what's the record for the most cats
in one tree?"

"When he doesn't like a new dog food,
I wish he would just sulk!"

"Never mind why—just put everything back, Sam."

"This must be serious!"

"Must you bring home discarded treasures
from the neighbor's trash?"

"I know his tail is wagging, but I'm waiting
for the message to reach his head!"

8·10
© 1983 United Feature Syndicate, Inc.

"But all he did was *sneeze*."

"Will you please find someplace else
to take a nap?"

"For the umpteenth time, *yes* you are
my best friend!"

"It's OK if you can't find the house keys...Marmaduke's been waiting for a chance like this to open the door!"

© 1983 United Feature Syndicate, Inc.

"Since you're new here, we'll let you go this
time...but don't ever call here again."

"He's like the kids...you can't tell him anything is *good* for him."

"I don't care if the scouts are having a
paper drive...I wasn't finished with mine!"

"He's *so* jealous...I have to give
him a squirt, too."

"Wow! Look at that cute French poodle
out there!"

"Good—here comes that bully who always picks on us when Marmaduke isn't here!"

"You should never have gunned your
engine at him!"

"He buries his bones deep now...last week,
one was missing."

"He's putting on his 'aren't I a wonderful pet?' act."

"I'm not hesitant to walk by Marmaduke
anymore...he's afraid of vacuum cleaners!"

© 1983 United Feature Syndicate, Inc.

8-27

BRAD ANDERSON

"Maybe he'll get tired and let us play with
our kite pretty soon!"

© 1983 United Feature Syndicate, Inc.

"Oh, stop it! You've been left home
alone before.

"Another first...we took a shortcut through
a carwash without a car!"

"Mom! Marmaduke's been hanging around
flea markets again!"

"No, I don't want to see what you caught!"

9-3 © 1983 United Feature Syndicate, Inc.

"I don't think Marmaduke is meditating
with us anymore...he's snoring."

"Don't worry...he just ate!"

"He isn't my *pet*, Marmaduke...he just
followed me home!"

"Try the siren...maybe that will wake
him up!"

© 1983 United Feature Syndicate, Inc.

9·8

BRAD ANDERSON

"Good dog! He shouldn't be watching that
kind of program, anyway."

"Can't stop to talk, Marjorie...
this is Marmaduke's supper!"

© 1983 United Feature Syndicate, Inc.

"Is he trying to tell us something?"

9.12 BRAD ANDERSON

"He's so happy when school starts...
it makes me sick!"

"That's some line he's got...showing them
his hubcap collection!"

"I never knew a pet could tie you
down so much."

"It isn't me he's excited about...it's my
leftover lunch!"

"You're watching 'Return of the Wolfman' again."

"Please...no more jumping for joy when you see another dog!"

© 1983 United Feature Syndicate, Inc.

9-19

"Easy, Buster...I'll do the driving!"

"I love dogs, but I don't think he
realizes that."

"Every time we have steak, he uses his
'ol' buddy' psychology on me."

"Don't read us a bedtime story. Tell us what happened when you walked Marmaduke today."

"He saw a bug!"

"How's 'King Tut' today?"

"You may have heartaches by the dozen,
but you're not going out!"

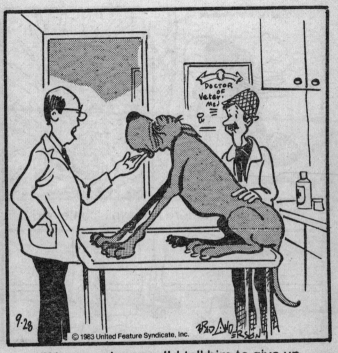

"If he were human, I'd tell him to give up wine, women and song."

"Watch this...before I can yell 'come and...

'get it'...it's gone!"

"Did you have to show off and make the
instructor heel?"

"Another wild party, eh?"

"One football nut is enough...but I've got *two*!"

"A Miss Bowwow is here to see you!"

© 1983 United Feature Syndicate, Inc.

10.5

"Every time he hears a noise, he has to get
in bed with me."

"Leaky roof!"

"How many times do I have to tell you?...
I don't work on Saturdays."

"Oh, brother! There are more dogs on the *other* side of the street!"

"Don't tell *me* both your legs are asleep...tell *him*!"

© 1983 United Feature Syndicate, Inc.

10-11

"Just close your eyes and you
won't see him."

"That's very nice, Marmaduke, but you still
have to go home."

"Well, he's partly right...you told
him to sit."

"I think we have a gas guzzler."

"Among other things...riding a skateboard
down Fourth Avenue."

"If you can convince him it's leftovers,
he'll eat it!"

"Frankly, I'm getting tired of being
squeezed out of my seat so Marmaduke
can spread out!"

10-20 BRADANDERSON

"Don't give him any cookies...we're trying
to break him of his begging habit!"

"Move over...we're having company!"